SOMEBODY

WHO

STORIES

GOLD WAKE

KNOWS

SOMEBODY

CHARLES RAFFERTY

For Wendy, Callan, and Chatham.
And for Scott Wolfman, of course.

CONTENTS

THE LIGHT MADE EVERYTHING
HARDER TO SEE

Tommy was on his way to the 7-Eleven to buy condoms. He had offered to use Saran Wrap and a rubber band, but Sheila wasn't game. They had just met and they had both been drinking, but apparently not enough. Tommy felt relieved when she suggested the errand. It would give him time to think, to figure out what he would say to Cheryl, his girlfriend of two years, when he saw her the following day.

It was warm outside and the deep snow was turning rapidly to fog, rising up to where Tommy thought the moon should be. He had put the porch light on as Sheila handed him directions, but by the time he got to the end of her long dirt driveway, the fog had swallowed it—or maybe, he thought, Sheila had clicked it off. The mountain roads made Tommy feel like he had wakened in a dark hotel room and couldn't find the door. He turned off the radio to keep his focus. When one of Sheila's rights could only be a left, he began to understand.

A yellow incandescence filled the air ahead of him. It was three road flares, leading to a car parked along a bend, its hazards flashing. A woman materialized, waving him to a stop.

"A car went over the side here," she said. "Do you have a phone?"

"I don't," said Tommy, patting his pockets even though he didn't own one. He got out of the car, and the woman backed away.

"You saw it happen?" he asked. He walked up to where the car had smashed through a wall of plowed snow and peered over the edge. The woman stood behind him, and Tommy wondered if she could smell the wine.

"I was following their taillights," the woman said. She looked up and down the road again as if more help were on the way, but it was after two in the morning. "I practically followed them right over."

As Tommy scanned the darkness, the woman kept chewing at a wad of gum. He thought she might be a little drunk herself.

"I could hear someone down there," she said. "But now it's stopped."

Tommy turned to her. He didn't like the idea of finding a car full of broken people. It reminded him of a terrible accident in high school, in which a baseball player had been decapitated, and the girl who was with him crawled halfway across a field of head-high corn to die in the moonlit rows. Everyone said that they'd been drinking, that the headless boy had his pants around his ankles. Tommy and the girl had been dating at the time. He believed he loved her and attempted to separate his outrage from his grief. For many days after, Tommy would not talk or listen to music. He preferred an iron silence.

"What's your name?" he asked. But the woman only handed him a flashlight, as if to say he was the man and he'd be going over the cliff to check on things now. Tommy clicked it on, but with so much fog, the light made everything harder to see.

Tommy turned, facing the darkness again, and called out to whatever might be down there. Something tiny came back to him. He couldn't say if it was a radio or a person or just some melted snow headed for the sea.

"How fast were they going?" he asked, kicking at a bit of sheered brush and noting a broken tree.

"Not real fast," she said. She took a pair of gloves from her coat pocket and put them on. "Maybe forty."

Tommy picked up one of the flares and placed it on the lip of the cliff so he'd have something to come back to. He knew he'd never make it to the 7-Eleven at this point, and the way back to Sheila's seemed impossible to trace. He imagined her finishing the wine and passing out, her body naked and untouched on the living room couch. Then he stepped over the edge, three-limbing it into the deep snow. He headed off in the direction he figured a slow moving car would take over a cliff like this, the height of which he had no way of judging. Behind him, the woman shifted her car into gear and pulled away.

After a couple of minutes, Tommy's shoes were soaked and the ground began to level. He looked up and could see the faint glowing of the flare. He called out again, waited, and heard nothing. He thought of Sheila's porch light and how it had disappeared. He thought of his old girlfriend crawling through the corn.

Tommy found a broken branch, then a hubcap lying on the snow like an LP record that had rolled across the floor. A smudge of moon showed itself high in the fog above him. His feet were getting cold now. Somewhere up ahead—and very close—he thought he heard a dead girl, singing.

THE CELLIST

He knew the lightest touch a woman could withstand before the air around her became a kind of music. That's what she told me about this man she used to date. That's why I'm taking lessons.

BOVINE AND DEFENSELESS

Martin loved to hear the electronic chime as he stepped across the threshold of Leather Junction—like one of those little xylophones the ushers tap in the lobby at the opera. He'd seen that in a movie once.

The chime made the girl behind the counter look up to meet his eyes, and it didn't matter if she immediately went back to pecking at her phone. He was satisfied with the human connection, however coerced or brief.

The store smelled deeply of leather. It was a good smell unless he thought about it. After all, it was the smell of skinned animals—bovine and defenseless. He had heard that, in the slaughterhouse, a giant sledgehammer came down and cracked the skull of each cow, that for many years, no one had thought to shield the cows further back in the line from seeing what was coming.

"What is it you're looking for?" asked the girl, brushing the blonde hair from her face and rising from her stool.

Martin scanned the boots and bomber jackets, and considered asking if she had any whips. But he was overcome by the iron in her gaze, the fact that her blouse could pass for lingerie. If he stayed, he saw himself destroyed by his own yammering, so he scooted back over the threshold and heard the electronic chime again. He saw how the girl stopped her advance, as if she would be punished for following, as if one of her anklets had the ability to deliver shocks.

Martin allowed himself to be swept up by the human stream pushing along the concourse. He knew that other stores had the same chime—Victoria's Secret, Barnes & Noble, Zales. He ducked into each of them as he passed—hearing the chime and waiting for a girl to approach him, before stepping backward into the crowded channel of the mall's upper deck.

Martin did a lap, and when he returned, Leather Junction was still empty save for the girl behind the counter. She was his favorite. He reasoned that, if he could avoid the chime, he could sneak up on her and read her nametag. He could get a sense of what she was really like, without her feeling the need to sell him the processed hides of cows. He could see the electronic eye about a foot above the tiles. One small leap and he'd be inside the store undetected, the twangy country music coming from the sound system just loud enough to cover his landing.

Martin took three quick steps and attempted to vault over the beam by placing his hand on a display table full of messenger bags. But the table gave way, and everything toppled. The back of Martin's head smacked into the floor like a bag of flour. The sudden commotion, in addition to the chime he had failed to avoid, brought the girl instantly from behind her counter. She had not seen his clumsy leap and could only assume he was having some kind of seizure, maybe even a heart attack.

"Should I call an ambulance?" she asked.

She was kind as well. He could see that now. She wasn't like the other girls who had dismissed him after their first glance. To them, he was practically invisible. He could bound out of an alley in front of them and they'd never break stride.

Martin imagined the weather inside the bell of her lavender skirt. It was leather of course, and he felt dizzy. He imagined the cow being peeled alive, its skin dipped into a vat of lavender dye, and stitched around the waist of the girl beside him now.

The blood was pooling beneath Martin's head, and for a moment he felt he knew what it was like to be one of her cows before it got turned into handbags. His vision was getting blurry, but he could still see the worry in her face. She was kneeling now, touching his shoulder. He could smell the perfume along her wrist mixed in with the pennies of his own blood.

"Can you hear me?" she said, with urgency.

He could just make out her nametag. Britney. The name of someone from the radio, of someone beyond his reach. Martin had no game, no way of charming her from the throne of his own incompetence. He wasn't even sure if he could speak. But he believed if he pretended to pass out—to stop breathing even—that she would have to lean in closer, and he was right.

THIS WOMAN WAS A LEOPARD

The spots were so smooth that Franklin wouldn't notice them if he closed his eyes and ran his thumb across her like he was testing a piece of furniture. They were the size of typewriter buttons, making her look like a leopard as she lay across the bed in the unforgiving light of the motel lamp. It was odd knowing this about her—this secret she kept buttoned away at the office. Even so, the message of her spots eluded him, and she seemed to be dissolving into the pattern of the bedspread, as if she were hiding in the grasslands outside Nairobi. Franklin drained the last of his wine. He felt the teeth inside her kisses, traveling down his neck.

FOR OFFICIAL USE ONLY

Marcus saw the station wagon pull away from the shoulder of Route 25, leaving behind a pile of fresh flowers in the snow. He was on his way to meet Trisha at her apartment. Trisha had separated from her husband, and a mutual friend had introduced them. Though they had met for an afternoon coffee two days before, this was their first real date.

The flowers were part of a roadside memorial. Someone had died there, and they had a lot of friends, a large and Waltons-like family. Marcus could tell this by the variety of bouquets and stuffed animals, the many tire tracks traced into the snow-covered grass.

Marcus made a snap decision. He hooked a left into one of those U-turns they have for cops and firetrucks. He saw the sign for official use only and he ignored it. He accelerated and took another illegal U-turn a mile up the road, and then he was headed back to the memorial, fitting himself into the tracks where the previous car had been.

He was outside for less than a minute as the traffic sped by, the drivers probably thinking he was one of the grievers, that he was saying some kind of prayer as he picked out the freshest and most durable of the flowers. And then he was back on the road, with an armload of calla lilies and orange mums. The whole thing was barely a hiccup. He wouldn't even be late.

People gave Marcus a funny look when he told them all this, but he didn't see anything wrong with it. Those flowers weren't doing David any good out there on the highway, he said. That was his name. Marcus saw it written in red spangles on several of the wire hearts. Apparently David was somebody's husband, and his wife wasn't ready to let him go. Marcus reasoned that the flowers would be destroyed the next day. Another storm was coming, and the plow would surely cover them as it scraped its way towards Bridgeport. David's friends and family had built the memorial too close to the shoulder. Marcus thought it might be on the very spot where David had died. Or perhaps they had simply lost all foresight in their time of flowers and grief. Either way, Marcus said, he didn't take them all.

When Marcus showed up at Trisha's door, she was surprised. No one had ever brought her flowers. She invited him in for a pre-dinner drink, but it was already clear to Marcus that they'd never make it to their reservation. The flowers had something to do with it.

Marcus liked the look of her as she stretched for a couple of highball glasses on the top shelf, and Trisha liked that he didn't turn away as her shirt rode up, exposing the small of her back. She held each glass up to the light, then ran them under the faucet to get rid of the dust. Their fingers brushed when she handed him the drink, and they ended up undressing each other right there in the kitchen. Marcus wondered aloud if he had to worry about her husband showing up, but Trisha told him she had switched out the lock last weekend. Afterward, they lay in a heap on the cold linoleum, laughing together, a little embarrassed. They decided to have their Thai food delivered.

Later, when Trisha fell asleep in the bed, Marcus pulled the newspaper from the basket beside her toilet. He found David's obituary and the write-up in the police blotter. Killed by a drunk was the main message. The drunk was fine, naturally. He sounded like Marcus—the same age, the same penchant for driving after the bar had closed. Marcus came out of the bathroom and made his way to the kitchen through the dark. He proceeded by a series of tiny steps, afraid that he might bump into something. He found the vodka bottle and poured himself a drink, downing it while listening to see if Trisha stirred.

Less than two weeks later, Trisha and Marcus were finished. They had had sex in a variety of positions and locations—a movie theater, a Stop & Shop parking lot, in every room of their two apartments. Trisha found out that he was allergic to shrimp and preferred tragedies to comedies. Marcus found out that she was still in love with her husband and didn't have a washing machine.

So they parted ways. Marcus remained the only man who had ever brought her flowers, and a snowplow destroyed David's memorial, just as Marcus had predicted.

SHIP INSIDE A BOTTLE

Her new boyfriend had a ship inside a bottle. You'd ask him how he got it in there, and he'd act like you had to be a Mason to hear the explanation. But really, you knew he must have bought it that way. He didn't know shit about getting a ship inside a bottle. It reminded me of those X-rays where you see a javelin stuck in somebody's skull, and you think, "Well how did that get in there?" It's just another story. Like Santa in the chimney. Like God in the wine. Like me inside her. Unlikely.

THE BLUE PIANO

"You boys are welcome to a beer," the old man said. It was a grudging offer, because we had scratched the piano as we took it through his garage. It was a small upright painted brightly, approaching azure. We took the beers.

"Myrtle would be glad to see this going to someone who wants it," he said as he clinked our bottles. "Music was everything to her." He didn't like that we didn't have straps, but Dave assured him by saying he'd ride in the back with it. The old man chugged his beer. When he went inside, we stood our bottles on the driveway, ducked into the cab, and left.

As I turned onto the highway, the piano shifted, knocking off two of its wheels on the corrugated bed of the pickup. This stopped it from rolling, and I could see the old man was right to worry. Still, we got it into the living room before Dave's wife got home. The piano was one of those big gestures he was prone to at the time.

But the instrument didn't sound right, and the piano

man told Dave the tune wouldn't hold for long. The pinblock had a crack in it.

Dave's wife played a couple of songs from her childhood lessons before the piano began to drift back to its earlier state, like a radio station that turns to static as you leave the city of its transmitter. By the following weekend, it sounded terrible once again.

The piano stayed in their living room for two years. They thought about fixing it, but the repairman told them it would be cheaper to buy a different piano if all they wanted was second-hand. "It's not like you're fixing up a Steinway," he said. "This thing has junk pile written all over it."

Whether the pinblock had cracked when we were transporting it, I couldn't say. We hadn't bothered to play anything on it before we loaded it up. Besides, the piano was free, and neither of us knew anything about music. It looked good in the living room though, despite the color, despite the lack of tune, despite the blue-painted blocks where the missing wheels had been.

Eventually the second call came. Dave needed my truck to get the piano to the dump. Out of a sense of obligation, I brought up Myrtle. Dave said he'd put an ad in the paper—"free to first-comer." But everyone who came knew something about pianos, and they always left after they peeked inside. It amazed him that they knew what to look for down in that nest of levers and wires.

So we brought it to the dump, and I took a video as Dave muscled it onto the concrete. A couple of people came over to watch. After all, how many times do you get to see a piano fall out of a truck? This one was quick. It cried out once with a chord of eighty-eight fingers and then fell silent.

Dave and I got back in the cab and cracked a couple of beers. By the time I dropped him at his house, the living room was already rearranged—a plaid couch filling the place where his wife would not make music.

SIX FINGERS

He had six fingers on each hand and played improvisational piano. The audience leaned in to hear his tinkling brook as it splashed around the fat stones of the double bass. The air at the club was dark and his hands were quick. Nobody noticed the extra digits. Later, at the after-party, a woman lingered beside his wine. She wouldn't have put it this way, but she was weary of the five-fingered world. She wanted to hear herself say the chords that only his hands could form.

THAT CUPOLA LYING ON ITS SIDE
AND COVERED IN VINES

Mason had never seen that gray shed behind the Busak's house tucked into some forsythia. He considered whether it might be new, but the shed seemed too at home among the branches. It must have been there all along.

Mason had begun noticing these things on rides with his daughter. He was teaching her to drive, getting her roadtime in before the big test. On Saturdays, she would pilot the car on all of his morning errands, and then, because it was enjoyable, they started going out together even if there were no errands.

At first, of course, he feared for his life. His daughter confused the brake and the gas. She drifted freely among the lanes without signaling. She got distracted by billboards and roosting hawks. But she was getting better, and the passenger seat began to fit him like a shoe. He found he could risk checking his email or focusing on the side window.

All his life Mason had been the driver. Although his wife was capable, she deferred to him automatically— whether it was a trip to New Jersey or to the liquor store. It had been like this for decades. Consequently, he never noticed that shed behind the Busak's. He never noticed that cupola lying on its side and covered in vines to the left of the Morris's swimming pool.

Now he was alert to it all but he had to refrain from commenting, for his daughter would crane her neck to see. The car would wander to whatever he had mentioned, and they might feel the rapid growl of the drift-protection grooves on the edge of the highway shoulder. So he found himself keeping to himself the fact that he saw three alpacas in the small fenced-in enclosure on the side of Route 34, that there was a woman in a startling red bikini walking around her pool as if there were a porpoise in there, slowly circling.

Mason enjoyed this small surrender, and he wondered what it meant, and where he was headed. He imagined, briefly, that he was really teaching her to drive him to his doctor appointments when he got old and decrepit. This is just one of the things he thought about with his daughter at the wheel, as he did his best to keep from her the things she must always have known.

NEIGHBORS

The houseplants in her window all turned brown. But it was winter and there wasn't any smell. It took warm weather to make us knock.

IT WOULD NEVER BE THIS CLEAN AGAIN

Christopher and his new wife, Molly, had moved into the tree-filled neighborhood two days before. They had always lived in apartments and didn't know a thing about yards. It was April, and as they stood at the picture window, feeling the sunshine warm their faces, Christopher realized he would have to cut the grass.

"Look at that big bird," said Molly. A turkey buzzard hopped along the border of the woods and lawn. Then she saw another.

"I think they're vultures," said Christopher.

When he opened the front door to investigate, the birds looked over at the sound of the whiny hinge, but they weren't ready to abandon whatever they had found. They ignored his approach until he was halfway to where they stood. Then they looked at the sky and took off. The birds were ungainly. It was like watching two copies of the Sunday *New York Times* attempting to take flight.

When Christopher reached the spot where they had

been, he found a black cat lying in the grass.

The cat must have been struck by a car. It wasn't broken in any obvious way, but the buzzards had made a couple of preliminary tears into the cat's asshole. Christopher looked up into the April sky. One of the buzzards was wheeling above the street; the other had settled on a branch two houses down.

The cat wore a pink collar with a brass tag. It belonged to the people across the street. Its name was Paws.

*

Molly sat at the kitchen table, pouring out wine for both of them.

"You can't just leave it there," she said

"Why not?"

"Because no one wants to come home and find their pet getting eaten by vultures," she said, rolling the wine dangerously close to the lip of her glass. "You have to let them know."

Christopher watched Molly walk to the window. The two birds were in the tree just above the cat. It was plain that others would follow.

"What am I supposed to do? Dig a grave?" He finished his wine and put the glass down on the stone counter with a clink.

A minute later, the first bird dropped down, and Molly handed Christopher a Hefty bag. She told him to get the shovel they had just purchased at Sears. When the birds saw Christopher coming, they each took another bite before setting sail above the neighborhood. He heard their wings beating at the flowery air as they departed.

Christopher had trouble balancing the cat on the shovel, so he picked it up by the collar, dropped it in the bag, and knotted it. The dead weight of it swinging as he walked felt indecorous, so he asked Molly to find one of the moving boxes they hadn't taken to the dump yet. He wrote "Paws" on the side, then tried to scratch it out. Dissatisfied with the result, he asked Molly for another box.

"I guess I'll bring it over when they get home from work," he said, placing the box at the end of his own porch, as if the UPS man had just delivered it.

Back inside, Christopher broke a head of lettuce apart under a running faucet. He felt the grit of the sand as the water sped over his fingers. Deep in the folds of the romaine leaves, he found a caterpillar stuck to the browned hole it had eaten through. He folded the leaf against the caterpillar, smashing it on the stainless steel of the sink basin, and washed it down the drain. He did not tell Molly about the caterpillar.

*

The grill was a house-warming present, and Christopher was pleased he'd been able to hook up the gas on the first try. He lay the thin, marbled steaks onto the pristine steel and regretted, for a moment, that it would never be this clean again. He thought of the grill he'd grown up with, coated with rust and chicken grease, and wondered how soon this one would become like that. Christopher checked his watch and went inside.

"They just got home," said Molly, pouring herself another wine.

Across the street, a man in his fifties got out of the car and carried a briefcase into the house. He looked old to Molly and Christopher, successful. "Get over there before he opens a can of cat food," Molly said.

"The steaks," said Christopher. "Three minutes a side."

"I'm on it," said Molly, and then took up position by the picture window to watch the handoff of the dead cat.

Christopher lifted the box and carried it birthday-cake style across the street. It was heavier than he thought it would be. He considered whether to cut across the lawn or walk up the driveway. He kept to the driveway.

Christopher placed the box on the porch railing, his left hand resting on top of it as he knocked. When the neighbor opened the door, he had a drink in his hand. It looked like scotch. Christopher explained that he lived across the street now, and when Bert (that was his name) opened the door to shake hands, Christopher had to step away from the box and it tumbled into the bushes.

Christopher smashed a couple of tulips as he clawed the box out of the shrubbery. He handed it to Bert with some ceremony, explaining that it contained Paws, that he had found him on his own lawn earlier.

Bert put his scotch down and pulled open the box. When he found the bag, he looked up.

"Vultures," Christopher said.

Bert tore open the bag, and the sight of Paws overtook him. He began to weep. Christopher would have backed away, but his exit was blocked by Bert, who was now on the porch, boxing him in against the railing. Bert explained they'd had the cat for 15 years, that they got him when they moved in, that now they were splitting up, that Paws was a point of contention.

"Where's your wife now?" Christopher asked.

Bert wiped his eyes and stood up straighter. "Sucking cocks in her new apartment," he said. "That's why I threw her out. I caught her sucking cocks."

Christopher could see he'd said the wrong thing, and he knew it was beside the point, but he kept thinking about "cocks." Had he caught her with two guys at once? Or had he caught her with different men on different nights? Or was he merely using the plural for effect?

"I would have done the same thing" was all Christopher could think to say.

Christopher stayed there with Bert until he was fully composed. It took a long time. Bert recounted how the cat had taken care of the mice that sometimes wandered into their home. He told Christopher how Paws had kept his feet warm during the winter months. Then Christopher helped Bert get the bag back into the box. He clapped him on the shoulder and worried that Bert might break down again. Eventually, Bert backed into his house and shut the door.

As Christopher headed over to his own house, he saw Molly staring at him from the front window. He could tell she'd been watching the whole time. She gave him a thumbs-up as she took a sip of her wine, which even from that distance appeared to be fully replenished. He wasn't sure if she was being serious or if she was poking fun at him for having dropped the cat into the bushes.

Behind their new home, gray smoke was billowing off the porch, and Christopher could tell that Molly had never turned the steaks, that the dinner they had planned was not the dinner they would eat.

THE FIRST SIGNS

In the new house, Ava was annoyed by the racket of the morning birds. We found frogs crawling over the vinyl siding, and Ava made me peel them off and throw them into the woods. The people before us had left a little garden. One morning, I stirred some of the chives into Ava's eggs. "How can you be so sure?" That's how she put it.

WHAT HAVE YOU DONE?

Mrs. Cartwright watched as I pulled the bouquet of wildflowers out of the passenger seat, holding it as if it were a child whose head I was protecting. She was standing behind the screen door of her front porch, halfway through the cigarette she smoked every afternoon before *General Hospital*. It was the first time I'd ever brought flowers to a girl.

"What have you done to my daughter?" she drawled. It was both accusatory and conspiratorial. She backed away from the screen, leaving me to pull the door out while cradling the sprawl of flowers. She held her cigarette off to the side and put her face into the bouquet.

"When a boy brings flowers, he wants something. When a man brings flowers, he's done something." She fixed me with her gray, laughing eyes. "Are you a man or a boy?"

"Is Julie home, Mrs. Cartwright?" I managed. I knew she was, but her mother would always finish her cigarette before she led me in.

Mrs. Cartwright didn't have a husband. It was never made clear, even to Julie, whether he'd run off or been killed. Mrs. Cartwright was a hard woman to read. Sometimes I worried that she would strike me, other times that she would kiss me. I watched as she ground out the cigarette in the ceramic ashtray that Julie had made for her in kindergarten.

"We should get those into some water, shouldn't we?" she said. She held open the door and tilted her head to indicate I should step inside.

Mrs. Cartwright produced a vase from under the kitchen sink. It was full of dust. "What do you think you're doing with these flowers?" she asked. She ran the vase under the tap, rubbing the dust away with the tips of her fingers.

"They're a present," I blushed. "Julie said she likes flowers." I had spent the morning gathering them from a meadow that bumped up against the Hollybrook Cemetery. It was such an armload that I was followed back to the car by bees.

Julie and I were both virgins, and the night before, in the parking lot of the Cherry Hill Mall, we had told each other that we were in love. We said it over ice cream. Then we kissed until our mouths hurt. We had no idea that such declarations often led to misery, believing as we did in the world's essential improvability. Julie told me I should get a condom, and when my father went to work that morning, I stole one from the box in the back of his sock drawer. I left it in the glove compartment of my car, beside the emergency flashlight and the owner's manual I had never found time to read.

Mrs. Cartwright set the vase between us on the counter and took the bouquet from my hands. She laid the flowers on the cutting board. "The last time Mr. Cartwright gave me flowers, he was trying to say how sorry he was for sleeping with a whore."

She said this looking directly into my eyes, so it was a surprise when the cleaver appeared in her hand. She brought it down on the bundle of stems, lopping off the bottom two inches. "All men want whores, eventually," she said, scooping up the flowers and arranging them in the vase—the goldenrod and turban lilies, the evening primrose and ox-eye daisies, the tight little pearls of an unopened flower I didn't know the name of yet. She fluffed them as if they were her daughter's hair, refilled her glass with chardonnay, and then called upstairs, "There's a boy down here for you, Julie. Better hurry up before he gets away."

I could hear Julie's feet rounding the landing and bounding down the steps. She had a ponytail and jean shorts cut high so the pockets peeked out on her toasted thighs. It was the kind of look that makes men drive into street poles. In a crowded room, she would have left a wake of longing. In this room, I felt the eyes of her mother upon me, and I pretended that Julie's beauty could not be seen.

"These are for you," I said, when her eye caught the flowers on the counter, brightening the kitchen like a strange fire.

Her smile widened and she stepped between her mother and me, moving toward the flowers, and I waited to hear whatever musical words might tumble from her lips.

Mrs. Cartwright cut in. "Loverboy here is trying to charm the pants off of you," she said, eyeing me through the bell of her upturned wineglass.

"Mother!" said Julie. "That's enough. Really."

"Yes. Really," said Mrs. Cartwright, as if Julie had asked a question. "Though I hope I raised you smart enough that you don't go off into the woods with the first boy who brings you flowers."

"Could we be alone, please," said Julie. "I think your show is on in the other room."

Mrs. Cartwright refilled her glass and smiled as sweetly as she could, saying "But of course, your majesty." Then she made an elaborate curtsy and backed out of the room, but her rump knocked into the door frame and she spilled some of the wine. Julie was still studying the ceiling, waiting for her to leave. So her mother made her face malevolent for me alone and drew her finger across her neck as if it were a bowie knife. Then she disappeared.

"Sorry about that," said Julie. "When she starts drinking, she's crazy."

"That's OK," I said, though it obviously wasn't. Julie looked like a full cup being carried too quickly. She seemed on the verge of crying.

"Some days I could just smother her in her sleep," she said.

Julie's jaw was clenched. Deep anger lines appeared on her forehead, and her eyes had the look of gasoline viewed by the light of a struck match. She marched over to the cleaver, picked it up in her fist and stood there looking at it. Then she dropped it into the clutter of the kitchen sink.

I wasn't sure what to say. I'd never seen Julie so worked up. She seemed dangerous, unpredictable. "I hope you like them," I said.

She whirled around and her eye landed on the flowers again. Suddenly her features softened. A smile broke across her face and brightened everything involuntarily. It was as if the angry Julie had been garroted as the smiling Julie rose up to take her place.

"What have you done?" she said slyly, slipping her hand into mine, as if I might be hiding something. And for the second time in the space of five minutes, I had no idea.

FLOWERS

We send them for birthdays and funerals, apologies and declarations of our sexual intent. The true aficionado disdains all flower-shop bouquets, and only the vainest among us prefers they be delivered at work. All other gestures fall short. A box of Belgian chocolates for the death of your son? A basket of fruit to carry down the aisle? Only cards are more widespread, but everyone knows cards are the poor man's flowers, the lazy man's. As you press your face into these tiger lilies, I want you to consider the labor I took to find this many perfect blooms in the meadow beside the highway, and then to climb through the downstairs window without waking the dog or your husband and leave them in the center of the dining room table—without chocolate or fruit, without so much as a card to tell you who I am or to say when I'll be back.

A BRIEF HISTORY OF MY RELATIONSHIP
WITH MERCURY

1. Becky and I woke up early to look for Mercury. The sky was mostly clear and unspectacular. The unrisen sun had just begun to taint the few clouds there were with the orange of overripe pumpkin. Several dim lights were present, and Becky asked which one was Mercury. I had no idea, but this did not stop me from pointing at the tiny speck about to be swallowed by a brightening cloud.

2. When I was nine, I dropped a thermometer on my bedroom windowsill. The mercury spilled into the track, and I didn't know that it was poison. I played with it for days—rolling it back and forth with my finger, shattering it, watching the ball bearings of it spread and recombine. A week later it was gone. The breeze that blew over my August sheets must have

found some way to hide it.

3. And there was Freddy Mercury, of course. I remember the autumn when "Under Pressure" was everywhere. Becky picked me up as I walked along the muffler-strewn shoulder of Route 38. We drove around all afternoon. That song came on at least four times, and every time we turned it up.

4. Mercury was both the most boring and the most exciting of the space programs. It ended before I was born. Somebody decided to sit on top of a weapon. Somebody decided to go to space and come right back. It reminded me of my father, who dove into the pool when he got hot enough but climbed right out, dripping over the copy of *War and Peace* he'd been working on all summer.

5. Becky drove a Mercury. We made out in it. There always came a moment, after we had parked and kissed for a while, when we would step out of the car and reenter through the back doors from our separate sides. It was like we were kids again—riding in the back, getting driven. The seats were cold at first. Vinyl. Easy to clean.

6. When I was little, I traded a Mercury dime for an Indian head penny. Mark Morris said I was a fool but it was worth it. I had a whole bag of the dimes, and my oldest coin was a 1923 Lincoln penny. Now I had an Indian head: 1898, and still the oldest coin in my collection.

7. The god of Mercury was supposed to be fast. He brought news that the king was dead, that the war was lost, that the girl you waited for was fooling around in the back of her mother's car.

HIS GLASSES

He preferred to keep them on. Even at the beach. Even as he waded to the point where his feet could not touch bottom. At night, as part of her seduction, his wife would take them off. Nothing was clear but her body above him, the stars beyond her drowned.

MEDUSA

Like most disasters, the snakes came all at once. I awoke to find the lover beside me turned to a wall of broken stone. One by one, the servants became rubble before my eyes as they answered my cries for help. Fear made me wise. I threw my mirror into the moat that I might stay a stranger to myself. Even the imperfect image of my face in a quick-running stream was enough to stiffen my joints.

The villagers do my bidding. They know that if my meals are not brought, I'll come down from this castle and look in all their windows, rapping slyly on the sill. When I'm in the mood, they bring a boy to me in blindfolds. As long as he does what I say, the snakes can be managed. I have learned the hard way that kissing is impossible. The venom works into his veins like molten tin, and when that happens, it's preferable to pull the blindfolds off. I let the boy decide.

I know what you're thinking—that the pretty girl has

turned ugly, that she likely had it coming. Maybe I did. Beauty begets enemies, and when it's gone, most women must take whatever passes for love. I'm here to tell you it's not impossible to live in two worlds well. There is another path and I am on it. Let no man dare mishandle me.

ROMANCE

Before they went into the bedroom, he opened a second bottle of wine and handed her a burgundy egg. The evening was hatching. A toad outside sat under the porch light, eating the moths that fluttered down, and the moon kept tearing at the clouds. Afterward, a breeze cooled over him wherever she had been, and the night birds had their say. He listened as he pretended to sleep, trying to recall where his shirt had fallen.

REGISTER 8

There's a funny smell around Register 8 and none of the cashiers want to use it, but it's Saturday, a couple of weeks before Christmas, and Maggie is stuck there.

Maggie is the cutest girl in Marshalls, and she worries people will think that she is the source of the smell. This is preposterous. The sight of her in the break room makes me think, unaccountably, of vanilla extract, of cakes leavening behind the little window of my grandmother's oven.

A menswear price-check comes over the PA, and because I'm in the pants section, I'm able to make it to the register more quickly than Adam, who is over in the dress shirts, straightening the rows. Adam has been hitting on Maggie ever since he got hired for the Christmas rush. Maggie and I are year-rounders, and the first thing I check on the schedule each week is when our times will overlap. To take a belt or a fleece jacket from her hand means the possibility of contact, of rapture.

"Can you get this for me?" she asks. It's an Oleg Cassini dress shirt. I know right away that it's $9.00 on clearance, but the customers don't like a quick answer. They think you're making it up. They want to see you go over to the shirt bins, find an identical shirt, hold them side by side, and nod. The cashiers like it this way too. It punishes the customer for being stupid enough to bring over the only Oleg Cassini dress shirt that doesn't have a price tag riveted to the center line of buttons.

"What does she need, dude?" says Adam, trying to see the tag on the collar, but I pull it close.

It doesn't matter. Adam is already scanning the bins. He knows the only peach-colored shirts we sell are Oleg Cassini. He walks down the opposite aisle, grabs one, and heads straight to the register. Adam is a real douche.

From the shirt bins, I watch Maggie give Adam the sleepy-eyed smile that makes me love her. It reminds me of the Rod Stewart song that is everywhere on the radio, and which every guy in the store is singing in his head as he approaches her. Then she looks at me as if to ask why I haven't brought the shirt back.

When I do, I hear Maggie telling the customer it's "awful" and that they "can't find the smell." She speaks loudly enough that the people at the end of the line hear it too. I hand her the shirt and fail to graze even the forlorn edge of her thumb.

Mr. Mortka can see that the line for Register 8 is half the length of any other, even though the store is full of customers. It's plain that people are trying to keep away. So when the store closes, Mr. Mortka calls me and Adam over. He tells us to find the smell and get rid of it.

"Don't clock out until you do," he says.

In front of each register is a display bin. The one in front of Maggie's is full of cheap pocketbooks, and there's a door you can slide open at the bottom to replenish the merchandise. We empty all of it, and Adam scans the inside with a flashlight. There's nothing there, so Adam says he'll try pulling the bin away from the register, which I didn't even know was possible. The bin is heavy, but we manage to push it aside.

When we do, the smell gets suddenly much worse. We can see that there's a slot between the bottom of the bin and the floor, a hidden compartment of sorts, and we can see lots of filth in there, which is probably mouse shit, but when we get on our hands and knees and shine the light in, we can see it's more than that. Dead mice are all over the place, mixed in with a nest made from socks and lacey underwear. Maybe there's a dozen of them, covered in what might be maggots.

"How the fuck did they get in here?" Adam says as he backs away, rubbing at his eyes. Across the store, I watch Maggie leaving with the guy from the shoe department, and I can see how her purse, hanging from a strap attached by golden buckles, bangs against her hip.

We get the mop, the heavy gloves, and a bag. At least we have found the source of the smell, so we don't mind scraping up the half-liquefied mice and scrubbing the floor with bleach. I'm surprised to see how hard Adam is working. Our only wish is to make the air around Maggie's register cerulean once again.

MY THREE-WAY

Our neighbor Bonnie had a lot of loud sex. To be fair, she tried turning up the stereo, but her boyfriend always pointed her right at our headboard. One night, Donna and I were making love while Bonnie was getting fucked. Bonnie came repeatedly on the other side of the wall, and hearing her, or knowing that I was listening, made Donna more vocal, more passionate. Bonnie, in turn, got louder still. But then, over breakfast, Donna denied having come with Bonnie, and that afternoon in the communal laundry, both of them kept quiet as they measured out their soap.

ROMULUS

It wasn't like that. Our mother suckled us for years in the rank, familiar den. She chewed the deer meat until it was a fine paste she could drop into our mouths. She must have wondered at our toothless gums, why our brothers grew so quickly. The one you call Remus was bigger. He took the first and last bite of everything we had.

By the time we could join our brothers on the hunt, our mother was in decline. It was I who brought her the entrails and shins. She lingered for weeks inside our den, nursing a paw that began to stink.

When winter came, the snow kept getting deeper. We could feel each other's ribs as we huddled in a knot at the bottom of our cave. The cold made it difficult to sleep, and I woke at odd hours. There, among the soft whining of my brothers, I stared out of the den's entrance as it floated above us like a cloud of stars.

We began to starve in earnest. One night I broke a path as far as I could, knowing the whole country was hungry, that something else would have to venture forth. I failed to catch anything but the scent of my own wandering, and I returned to find our mother disassembled, the muzzles of my brothers bloody. I was too weak to rebuke them, and they made it clear the marrow was theirs. It was Remus whose belly sagged most heavily.

Whether I fled or was driven out I cannot say, but the shepherds found me. My first memory of them was waking to food made better by fire, the pleasure of blankets. They gave me a new language, and I was amazed at its precision, that the dogs obeyed so readily. In time I could express the exact shade of my gratitude and my despair.

I tried my hand at herding, but I was better at building dens. They called them houses, huts, granaries, barns. I caused one to rise where their own was falling down. I built another one beside that, only better. I had a knack for making stones lock into each other, for thatching a roof that could keep out any weather.

Soon other men arrived on our grassy hill. They marveled at the clarity of the Tiber and how it never made them sick, so I constructed an aqueduct that diverted the river to a field they were filling with grapes. I showed them how to pave the roads that connected us all like rope. Everything rose, became sturdy, could be seen for many miles. They said it was a city. They said I was its king.

When our crops failed, we gathered our spears and conquered the people to the north of us. We murdered the men as they knelt beside their flocks. We slaughtered their sheep and roasted them whole over the burning rafters of their homes—for hunger and loyalty can never coexist. Then, because the crown fit snugly upon my head, we took their women back with us, ignoring their tears and all that they implored. It was a long time before I understood what I had done and why I was so hated.

Some nights, I step alone onto the palace steps—with a bowl of wine and the smell of my wife all over me, my daughters and my sons asleep on their many pillows—and I listen to the pack gathering in the hills. Most of the old voices have dropped away, and I imagine the sad feast that must have attended each dead brother. I understand now how hunger joins us, how I would have had my fill if the neck was warm and waiting.

One call in the darkness is unlike all the others. This is Remus. I can feel him staring down into my lighted windows, regretting our mother, knowing I will kill him if he ever attempts to warm himself in the triumph of my bed.

I think of him often—full of worms and rancid deer, a grin of loosening teeth—maneuvering his way to the center of the sleeping pack. We are old now, and the two of us are dying surrounded by stone, I of the palace and he of the den. But the same stars salt our sky.

Ah, Remus, I forgive you for nothing, and I hope that you can bear it.

INHERITANCE

A young man's apartment complex burned. He stood in the parking lot watching, holding only a bird cage with a single parakeet hopping from perch to perch. Then the crisis passed and he married a woman. They had children. They took some trips. Then his wife ran off, ushering in a new crisis that also eventually passed. Many years later, the man died of something common. I don't care what you say. Even after the parakeet was put down by the vet, I'm sure he kept the cage. His children found it as they were cleaning out the house and, at the urging of the realtor, took it to the dump.

THEN I FELT THE FLOOR BENEATH ME

Nancy was due in a month and the tech company I was working for had just laid off most of the pretty girls. It was 2001—just after the Mir space station fell into the ocean but before the attacks on the Twin Towers. The company wanted to boost morale, to see if we could "reboot" ourselves and start making money again. So on a Friday night in April, we were treated to drinks and Chinese acrobats. Spouses were welcome, and we headed to Manhattan in style, aboard three charter buses.

Nancy and I sat behind Evan and his wife, Marna. Their first child was one-year-old and they were grateful for a night in the city. They had gotten a sitter and were overdressed—he in a blazer and tie, she in a scarlet cocktail dress with spangles along the neck.

"You'll love it," Marna insisted. "Evan was there to cut the cord. It was the most fulfilling day of our lives."

Every couple we encountered told the same story— how the last trimester was their favorite, how the blood and uncontrollable urination of the delivery brought them closer. Nancy, on the other hand, was sleepy and putting on weight, and I had taken to buying Tums with my cigarettes. It was a scary time. Nancy had lost her job, and my own company seemed suddenly unhinged. We had just laid off a hundred people, and now we were passing bottles of scotch up and down the aisle of a charter bus.

"There's nothing more rewarding than cleaning my son's bottom," said Marna. I looked over at Evan, but his eyes shone with earnest agreement. Nancy pinched at my arm.

"I just hope the seats in the theater are comfortable," said Nancy. "Whenever we go out now, I just want to sit."

"I can't remember the last time we were out, the last time we did something romantic," said Marna. She made it sound like they'd been living in a gulag.

"Daniel and I always make time," said Nancy. "You know what he did for me once? He took me to look at the Mir as it flew overhead?"

"That Russian thing?" asked Marna.

"It's when we were first going out. Back in college." She took my hand as she spoke but the others couldn't see this. "Mr. Science here brought me out by the lake one night to have a look."

"Sounds like a cheap date," said Marna. Then she turned to Evan to ask for the name of a movie she'd forgotten.

The theater, it turned out, was on a street too narrow to accommodate our buses. We got stuck halfway down the block when someone's car was parked too far out from the curb. We couldn't get by and backing out would take too long. We would have to walk.

"I hope it's not far," said Marna. "It'll be murder in these heels." She stuck her foot into the aisle so we could see the frail stiletto. It looked as though it would turn to splinters beneath Nancy.

When we arrived at the theater, a man with a tiny xylophone was already walking around the lobby, hammering the keys and asking people to head into the performance space. We were allowed to take drinks inside as long as the containers were plastic and had a lid, so I ordered two scotch and sodas at the intermission bar, and a cranberry juice for Nancy.

"It's too bad you can't have one of these," Marna said to Nancy. Then she took a sip of red wine through a tiny straw.

The theater was dark and cramped. A mix of late eighties metal bands blared from the sound system—Mötley Crüe, Dokken. The black lights were on and everything was glowing as though someone had detonated many cans of fluorescent paint. Bits of bright confetti fell through the air, sifting from some perch up in the rafters. Just as I noticed there wasn't any seating, a voice came over the sound system and said we were free to mill about. I rolled my eyes in sympathy with Nancy.

High above us and without ceremony, acrobats in glittering unitards began walking across wires we couldn't see. They somersaulted, they leaped, they swooped like hungry birds. Others built strange gravity-defying structures out of their bodies on the floor beside us. They encouraged us to come as close as we wanted. As I drained the last of my scotch, I remember thinking it was amazing they hadn't crashed into each other—or into one of us. Nancy leaned over and said she was going to the ladies' room. The lights were making her dizzy and she needed to sit down.

I watched as the door closed behind her, and then suddenly, spotlights began swirling over the entire crowd like deranged seagulls until eventually a dozen separate lights converged on my face in a blazing circle. Everyone started cheering as the Chinese acrobats took hold of me. They made me step into a harness. Wires were produced from somewhere up above and they began attaching them. I told them that I was afraid of heights, but it was clear they didn't speak English. Then Marna, smiling, pushed me into the orange arms of one of the lady acrobats. A small green man took the empty scotch containers from my hands and floated upward.

Everyone was chanting my name as I slowly rose into the black rafters of the theater. The orange lady let go of me, and somehow, the acrobats began circling me like frogs or angels. It felt like I was caught in some kind of reverse whirlpool. It reminded me of a bad acid trip I'd had in college, and it was happening in front of the people who could fire me. I shouted for it all to stop, but the music only increased, and I saw my coworkers getting smaller as I swung back and forth above them until finally I had reached the very apex of the theater. Glowing acrobats hurried along the catwalks getting ready for the next set of leaps.

The scotch was affecting me badly. I worried that the thin wires would snap, that I would plummet to the floor, that I would pee myself as I died in a heap in front of the last good-looking woman in accounting. I held on as tightly as I could, but I was basically holding onto myself.

Then the music paused, and the spotlights again

swirled in like a bunch of hungry gulls and came to a rest all over my body. The music began building as if some unstoppable grand finale were already underway. I yelled again, but it blended into whatever the guitars were saying. I was rising and falling, rising and falling, and I couldn't see anything with the spotlights in my face. It was like they were trying to break me, to make me believe that I could die, that the wires that held me might as well be whiskers. For a moment, I thought about the Mir tumbling into the ocean, how it would have felt something like this if a cosmonaut had been left onboard by accident—waking to find himself hurtling to his doom. I couldn't tell if I was sideways or right-side up. And then suddenly, impossibly, there were hands all over me. They guided me downward, and then I felt the floor beneath me.

I searched the crowd for Nancy as the Chinese acrobats stepped me out of the harness, but I was still blinded by the spotlights. Then, amid the pounding music and the drunken back-claps of my coworkers, I felt what must have been Nancy's hand in mine, and I resolved to follow it wherever I was led.

AN INABILITY TO FOCUS

When she asked if Jerry had protection, he showed her the black square of the Trojan. It had been in his wallet for so many months it looked like the wrapper was concealing a monocle. It didn't seem trustworthy in the dim light of her dorm room, and he thought about how dumb the name "Trojan" was. After all, the Trojans were responsible for the most famous security breach in all of literature. Calling a rubber a Trojan was like naming an airline Nosedive. Jerry's uncle had died in a plane crash. Jerry had forgotten the fact until that moment, and although he had never met this particular uncle, he was a piece of family lore handed down. There a picture of him on his mother's piano. Incredibly, Jerry's uncle was wearing a monocle in the photograph. That just didn't happen anymore. Could it have been a joke? Could the fashions have shifted that drastically in just a single generation? And why was Jerry thinking of airline disasters and eyewear while the woman he'd been pining after for so many weeks was finally causing him to lose altitude above the snowfield of her skin?

SOUDERVILLE

The news came on and he turned it off. It was eleven o'clock, and the streets of Colby were quiet. Whatever was lit up had been forgotten or left on out of habit. He paused at a red light beside the bridal shop, where the windows were full of mannequins in prom gowns and taffeta. He tried to remember the last time he'd felt taffeta.

The light changed and he lurched forward beneath the sagging Christmas decorations, the festoons of electric candy canes. He had lived in Colby until he was sixteen. Then he moved away. It was the summer that promised to teach him about girls, but he was forced to wait, to start over in a city that didn't know him. Now he was 43 and had a job that took him through his boyhood town.

The river to his left was fat and silent. It made itself known only by the lights that reflected there. They were tall and fell apart across its blackness. The water would be icy this time of year. He wondered if he could make it across before succumbing to the cold and the current that moved eternally over its bed like a kind of sky.

He was coming back from teaching grammar at the community college. His students were all ex-fuckups—people that had flunked out of regular college or been to jail or gotten pregnant too soon. Now they were getting their second chance, but they had little patience for his grammar. The night's lesson had been about the subjunctive mood—the verbs that are based on wishes and desire. It was hard to explain the difference between "It's important that he love her" and "It's important that he loves her." He wondered if he understood it himself.

The empty road moved up and away from the river. He passed the stripper bar where once he'd seen a woman throw up on stage and keep on dancing. The neon lights were flashing, one car tucked in behind in what counted for discretion. He passed a row of houses, each with one room flickering and blue with television light. He passed the Apollo Restaurant, which had burned down that summer and never got rebuilt, never even got cleared away. He could smell it in the air whenever it rained.

The road returned to the river, and he drove across the dam where the water backed up into the mountains to swallow the town of Souderville. At the bottom the town still stood: a couple of streets, a few undemolished houses, a clothesline with the shirts still waving in the current, as if someone might come back for them after all these years. He knew a diver who'd seen it. He said they just left everything when the government paid them off—took the money and moved to higher ground. That was during the Depression. Now there was talk that the dam might not be safe, that it might fall down if they didn't tear it down first.

His own house was pinched into a cookie sheet of land

between the water and the surrounding hills. He couldn't see his house from where he was now. It was on the river part of the river, not the lake part that sprawled behind the dam. The river slid right past his bedroom window. Mostly it never made noise. But once, he'd been walking in the woods above his house and heard a small hiss that got louder as he marched over the new snow. When he came to a ridge, he saw it was the dam releasing water through one of its giant drawbridge doors—as if the castle were storming the countryside. It went on for hours and still the town of Souderville lay sleeping in the green and fishy light.

There had been a girl a long time ago, and he thought of her sometimes as he sped toward his wife, banking the car over wet roads that reflected almost nothing—his "check engine soon" light orange as a cigarette tip beside his left hand, the dashboard clock blinking the wrong time because he hadn't reset it after the battery failed, back in July. Mostly he thought about her voice, the way it had drifted into his ear each morning with the sunlight and the birds. She had a beautiful body, and she'd done beautiful, dirty things with it. Why didn't he think of that? Why didn't he think of the time she'd been a bridesmaid and he'd unwrapped her like a blue taffeta present back at the hotel room?

The lights were all out when he pulled into the driveway. There was no moon, and the February stars shone like bits of crushed blue glass. It reminded him of a street after an accident—the safety glass that tells the world something went through a window at high speed. His wife had seen a boy go through a windshield when she was very young. When he asked her if the child had lived, she didn't answer because the question, he later realized, was ridiculous.

Inside, the dishwasher was whining through its cycle. His daughters' room was dark. He could hear them breathing through the cracked door, but he didn't risk pushing it wide or flipping a switch.

His wife was sleeping too. The remote control rested on the quilt where it had slipped from her hand as the local news played over her, talking about the murders and fires in their part of the world. "He lived in this house," the on-the-scene reporter was saying. "A quiet man well-liked by everyone he knew."

He turned it off. It was the same disaster they'd been talking about all day—a man who killed his family and set the house on fire with him and everyone else inside. The man wouldn't surrender and he shot at the firemen who tried to help, so they hid behind their trucks and let it all burn down.

This was the world he lived in now. People misunderstood the language of desire. Men killed their families. Rivers backed up over entire towns. And the women we loved disappeared. Even though we married them, even though they looked as if they tried to wait up in hopes of our safe return.

RHODODENDRON

Once again, the rhododendron had failed to flower. She wanted him to dig it up and put it in the backyard where the light was better, but four years had passed since he'd planted it beneath their bedroom window. He said it was too late, that the roots had spread and sewn it into place. She said she didn't believe him, that he should have listened when they'd first driven home from the nursery. She walked to the shed and got the shovel. He went inside and poured a drink. Through the kitchen window, he saw his neighbors' rhododendrons exploding. He imagined the many bees pushing to the bottom of each blossom. He imagined what it must feel like to pull into the driveway and step through the cursive of their plenty. Then, out back, he heard his wife's heel stomping into the shovel.

MARY AND BERNARD:
A CAUTIONARY TALE

On their first night together, as Bernard achieved orgasm, he began to bellow like a charging rhinoceros. Mary worried that he was having some kind of seizure, that she might have to twist her way free of him and call the paramedics. But then it passed, and because they had both been drinking, Mary decided that sleep was preferable to any investigation of the noises Bernard had made.

When it happened a second time, she was sober and laughed out loud. She thought he must be kidding or, at the very least, playing things up for the camera that was pointed at her bed—not much different, really, from her own uncharacteristically vocal participation. Of course, Bernard attempted to go along as if it were all a joke, but Mary could tell from his shamed eyes that the rhino sounds had been involuntary, that she had mocked what for Bernard had been sublime.

Mary didn't like that look in her man's eyes, and she resolved to banish it from her bedroom. She had been with other men who had sexual quirks—the spankers, the handcuffers, the silk aficionados, the ones who liked to taste what would otherwise be private.

So Mary learned to accept the rhinoceros sounds whenever they welled up. Another man might whisper "oh God"; this one snorts like a rhinoceros. It was all quite simple. But then, because Bernard did not make the rhinoceros sounds every time, Mary began to miss them. She saw their lovemaking as a failure if he denied her this audible proof of his enchantment.

So Mary spent a lot of time trying to coax out of him the high-pitched whines and suffocated grunts, but it didn't always work. In fact, Bernard was making the sounds less often. For him, it was no great matter. The sex was athletic and fulfilling whether he made the sounds or not.

But Bernard was a considerate lover. He began to wonder: Does a meal taste better simply because the knife and fork can be heard against the good china? He could tell that Mary needed the rhino sounds the way some men needed their wives to dress up like a French maid on Saturday nights. He decided he could fake it for Mary.

The next evening, after Mary finished her second glass of wine, Bernard turned off the light and began kissing her neck. It wasn't long before they were off to the races, as they say, and Bernard began serving up some low-decibel growls. Mary slowed down. She could tell that something was amiss, but Bernard continued with his script until he arrived at a kind of lewd trumpeting.

It was all for nothing. Mary had detected the fake. She felt like a girl who had just been given a plastic corsage. She said it was an insult and sent him packing to the couch downstairs, hoping all night that he would come back up with a true and open heart.

Their relationship went downhill after that. Mary began questioning the veracity of all Bernard's previous rhinoceros noises. Could he have been fooling her all along? Was the temple of their sexual satisfaction built on a foundation of sand and poorly rendered zoo sounds?

What followed were days of darkness. Mary refused to take his calls, and she fell deeper into depression. She could not fathom why she had grown so dependent on these noises. What if, at the moment of ecstasy, he had made crow sounds instead? Or begun talking like Nixon? Or whistled the Andy Griffith theme? Would she still be pining away like this? Sadly, she knew the answer was yes. Bernard was not just any man. He was the one. She could admit that now.

Mary resolved to take action. She went to visit Bernard at his apartment unannounced, wearing only high heels and a trench coat. It was a fantasy Bernard had confided in her once, and she was determined to rekindle their romance.

But what was that? When she got to his door, she heard the rhino sounds coming from inside the apartment. Was Bernard conducting an affair? Was she a fool to think they were exclusive? Was it possible to lose oneself this completely while masturbating?

Alas, Mary would never find out the answers to these questions. She accepted that the relationship had run its course and felt the cruel wind of November rising up beneath her coat as she tried to flag down a cab.

Meanwhile, inside, oblivious to everything, Bernard tilted up his beer and continued watching the National Geographic special, about the touch-and-go future of the African rhino.

FLING

She was a cliff. He was confetti. Why not?

COLONEL SANDERS IN EXTREMIS

Colonel Sanders stood outside using the glass door like a mirror. He straightened the black necktie and brushed a bit of lint from his sleeve. "Fucking white suit," he said. Then the old man cleared his throat and entered the restaurant door, which he shed like a magician's handkerchief. He became the smiling grandfather, full of good will and good chicken. A five-year-old boy saw him first and hid behind his mother's leg. It was a good spot, Colonel Sanders thought, like crouching behind a plaid oak stump.

"Thank y'all for coming to try my chicken," he intoned. His voice did a good job of filling the room, but few people made eye contact. Sometimes it was like that.

Johnson came up from behind and practically goosed him. "Work the crowd now, Colonel, work the crowd," he said, as he sailed over to the condiment island and began replenishing the napkins.

"Johnson can suck my old gray cock," the colonel

thought. Then he paused to make sure his face still fit the mask of the southern gentleman, the man with the secret recipe. "My chicken is always crispy," he croaked. "I do declare."

The women were more tolerant of his presence than the men. He knew it would be otherwise if he was just playing at being old. But he was 79 that month. No need to bleach his goatee white, no need to add gravel to his voice. He sidled up to a young woman in her thirties. She had large breasts, which is what the colonel liked best. "Well that chicken looks finger-lickin' good," he said as he stared into the half-devoured bucket she was sharing with her friend. He circled around to see if he could sneak a peek down the undone buttons of her blouse. "Those thighs look delicious."

"Why thank you, Colonel," she said, giggling to her friend.

The men could be cruel, and it was unnerving how often they zeroed in on the goatee. He had worn it for decades. It's what got him the acting job. "Do the ladies like the feel of that goatee as they're sittin' on your face?" they'd ask. "Your sister liked it mighty fine" was the answer that got Johnson to report him, but there were no backup colonels to be had, and so, as with most things, there were no repercussions.

Johnson looked up from the now fully loaded napkin dispensers and twirled his finger in the air beside his face. It was the signal every store manager used to convey that Colonel Sanders needed to keep moving around the dining area. The colonel headed to the next table, but only to try his luck with the large-breasted woman from a different angle.

The colonel was on loan from corporate. He spent an hour a day at six different KFCs in the Hartford area. It was a publicity stunt, though "stunt" wasn't the right word. It had all the agility and surprise of a body double losing his balance and hitting one branch after another as he plummeted to the ground. When his hour was up, he'd get into a van shaped like a fried chicken leg, and head to the next KFC.

"KFC," he thought. "Why did they change the name? Goddamn initials! Do people want IBM to make their dinners?"

When he was done interrupting meals and leering at the women, he left without saying anything to Johnson. He was pleased to know he'd never have to see his pimply neck again. Out in the parking lot, the colonel snuck a smoke beside the dumpsters. He'd already been reprimanded for smoking in the van, but he refused to give it up entirely. His departure routine also included a swig of whiskey.

Finally, before he got into the van, he took out a handkerchief and cleaned his glasses. His eyes were still good, so headquarters had given him a pair with flat lenses. He was forever having to wipe the dandruff off of them. He considered popping the lenses out, but he had heard they check for that. The whole point of the promotion was to let people meet a real Colonel Sanders. Everything had to be authentic, which is why he didn't feel bad about splurging on the flask—stainless steel, with a rifle and a dog etched into it across a silhouette of Kentucky. He filled it each morning with sour mash. "Something befitting a colonel," he said to himself.

On the way to the next restaurant, he got caught in

traffic. It happened every day. People were always honking and pointing, laughing at the half-broke actor who hadn't planned well for retirement. On this occasion, he got mooned by some Catholic schoolgirls headed home on the bus. That part he didn't mind. They were all cute, and their smiles were both wanton and chaste. He believed their future was bright.

Colonel Sanders pulled into the last KFC of the day. In fact, it was the last stop of the entire promotion. He had half a flask of whiskey left, and he drained it on the spot. "Let them fire me," he said out loud. It was dinnertime on Friday, just outside of Cheshire. He was a little late, and the manager met him in the parking lot. "Come on now, Colonel. Let's get moving."

"I got caught on 84," he said in his native, New Jersey voice. It was an effort, sometimes, to speak the way he'd been born. Even when he wasn't wearing the suit, he felt the drawl creeping into his voice. The campaign had been going for two straight months, weekends included, and he felt like he was living the part. Of course, he could never get away with his Sanders voice in the actual south. Corporate had real southern gentlemen for that. But here in Connecticut, the diners never questioned his adopted voice, even though he had arrived at it simply by trying to sound as stupid as possible. He imitated the woman from Georgia who lived in the apartment beside his own. She was forever screaming at her kids about their lice and the loud TV. She said things like "hoppin' mad" and "crooked as a dog's hind leg." He tried to use these expressions when he was in character. He was an actor, after all, and he knew that every role required study—however small, however meager the recompense.

Inside the restaurant, a small crowd was waiting for him. The women all had children, and a couple of flashes went off as he came through the glass door. "Well, well," he said. "Looky what we have here." He said this last word in two syllables. It was the kind of exaggeration that would get his ass kicked in Kentucky, but here among the Yankees, it went unremarked. To them, his accent was just as good as the clothes, and the clothes were authentic. Initially he worried they would make him wear polyester, like the cooks and cash register girls. But he was a man apart. His costume had to be dry-cleaned—and they made it clear that it was his bill to pay. It was for this reason he never ate the chicken they sometimes offered. It was just too messy and he was always in a rush. What did he care about a ten percent discount anyhow?

Colonel Sanders shook hands with the toddlers, and paid extra attention to the kids with good-looking mothers. He was feeling the whiskey now, and he asked if they might have any questions, figuring he'd get the same old stuff about the secret recipe and where his first store opened. He had memorized all the answers off a laminated sheet taped to the dashboard of the chicken leg van.

One kid called him Captain Sanders, and he corrected him. "I'm a colonel, my boy. A colonel from the south!"

Another kid piped up: "Were you in a war?"

"Why yes I was, son. Yes I was."

"Was it the Civil War?" he asked, and a small tittering arose among the mothers.

"No, no, no," he pretend-laughed. "I was in the Korean War," which he pronounced as "KO RE un" in his pretend accent, realizing as he said it that he had broken character. He whipped around to see if the manager had caught it.

71

"Did you have to kill any Koreans?" a boy of about 8 asked, pronouncing the strange new word exactly as the colonel had.

"Bobby!" hissed his mother. "That's not polite." She gave his shoulder a pinch as she held onto him, and it was plain he got the message—he looked like he might even cry. Colonel Sanders usually couldn't be bothered with such children. But the boy's mother was practically falling out of her blouse, and he admired the blush that spread across her bosom. Plus, she was wearing yoga pants, and Colonel Sanders was curious to see what she looked like from behind.

"That's alright, my dear. The young'uns always ask the most pointed questions. Their innocence commands them!" He liked the way that last part sounded, especially with the accent.

In point of fact, Colonel Sanders had killed people in Korea. On several occasions, he had fired into throngs of charging enemy soldiers, and though he shot wildly, he had always assumed that some of his bullets hit some of the people headed toward him with silvery bayonets. The only person he was sure about, though, was when he had checkpoint duty. A woman was running toward him one night, as if she were scared of something, but he worried that she was a saboteur. When she didn't stop on his command, he shot at her. The third bullet took her down twenty feet in front of him, and the fear he felt made him keep shooting. He was a private at the time, and she turned out to be just a girl. Maybe 15. He still remembered the feel of her destroyed shoulder as he dragged her onto the stretcher. He didn't even get a reprimand for screwing that one up.

"There are no good choices in war, son," he drawled. He was feeling the full effect of the whiskey now, and he stumbled against an empty chair. He started to get misty, standing in the middle of the dining room, surrounded by the town's soccer moms, a toddler in every lap. He wasn't actually crying, but it was enough to ruin everyone's appetite for the extra-crispy special they had going.

And then, because he was tired, and because he was suddenly very drunk, he said in his real voice—his cynical, New Jersey, know-it-all voice—that men go to war despite the shame and the terror, because they believe the women they leave behind will remain faithful to them, that they won't take up with men who have bone spurs and heart murmurs.

"But expecting women to keep their legs crossed is folly," he said. "Sheer and utter folly."

The manager was staring at him now, drawing a finger across his own neck to make it clear that the colonel should shut the hell up. Despite everything, Colonel Sanders recovered himself. He was a professional after all. He forced the drawl back into his voice and began to say farewell as the women collected their children and hurried for the door. He took a last lingering look as they departed. It was touching how they had arranged themselves, like they were the audience, like they were watching a little play. Now they avoided his eyes, and some of them seemed to pity him, which was a foreign and not altogether unpleasant thing.

The women had looked delicious as they sat there listening. They were yet another thing he would not have time to taste.

BECAUSE HE HAD BEEN CRYING

He had dressed in the dark, and when he got to the car, he saw that he'd put her T-shirt on by accident. He looked up at her bedroom window then, and she was watching to make sure. It was a habit she had: She kept her thumb on the handle until the toilet finished; when she sprayed a wasp nest, she knocked it down and ground it out with her heel. And so he drove away, knowing that his own shirt was already in the trash.

THE ONE I RAN DOWN ON SUGAR STREET

I used to tell people I wasn't speeding. I'm sure now that was a lie. Every morning since, I'm going 40 in a 25 by the time I get to the spot where my car rolled over the fawn, tossing coffee into my lap.

I had just turned onto Sugar Street in the black August morning, headed for the train station, an interview, a new direction in my recently ruddered life. I hadn't had a drink in 62 days, and my wife had unpacked her suitcases to see if it would stick.

By the time I jammed the brakes, the worst had already happened. In the rearview, the fawn wobbled up, lit by a full moon falling, and hobbled unsteadily into the nearest yard. In the street was a smear of something wet—blood, urine, I wasn't sure. I could see the spots on its coat though, and from the other side of the road, the doe stood watching.

I got out to see if the deer had broken a headlight or crumpled anything important. Except for the mother deer bounding off in the opposite direction, it was quiet. There was a swamp nearby, but it was mostly exhausted in the predawn hour. There was none of the song and hustle of early evening. The fawn had likely been born in the woods beside it, and had probably drunk from it every day of its eggshell life. Everything looked fine, and I got back in the car and drove, listening for knocks and broken metal, something out of place.

I knew the fawn could not possibly have withstood my car rolling over it. It was surely down again by now. I could only hope that it made it to some woods.

I remembered another deer. It had died in our yard—right by the sandbox where our daughter played. When she found it, she ran up to pet it, but the summer flies undeceived her. We hired a backhoe to bury it ten feet further away in the tiny woods that ran between the houses like a moat of poison ivy and black cherry trees that turn the bird shit purple for two weeks in July.

And I recalled another time when my daughter's necklace got caught in the seat of a city bus. We were late. I gave it a firm yank and it came free, but without the charm—the dangling ice skates that might have been silver, or maybe just tin. We hurried off the bus and made it to the fair before it closed. I won her an orange crocodile that she still keeps at the foot of her bed. But the necklace—that's long gone. Which only proves my point. That something has to be lost, or destroyed outright, to make room for something better.

And then I was at the station, forcing dimes into the meter and hurrying to the platform, even though I'd beaten the train by minutes. Its headlight was still far up the track, its chugging as insubstantial as a song in somebody else's head.

Do I need to say that I got the job, that my wife decided to stick with me, that my daughter could build her castle without worrying that something would crawl up from the road at night to die in a stinking heap?

That deer was a sacrifice—the one I ran down on Sugar Street. I believe that everything would have gone against me if I didn't roll over it on the morning of my interview. I don't know why. I would have made the train regardless. And the black coffee in my lap was invisible in the navy blue weave of my trousers. But something had to pay for what I needed, and this time it wouldn't be me.

Every day at lunch, I sit in my office overlooking the Long Island Sound. I eat a salad, a piece of fruit. Almost all of the boats are at anchor. Sometimes I wonder what the other driver got for the deer he killed, and whether he knows that's why.

PEACOCKS

That summer, two peacocks showed up in the neighborhood. Jonathan and Karen listened to their cries at dusk, practically human, calling from one patch of woods to the other across their yard. It sounded like both a warning and a plea. Of course, in the beginning, they didn't know it was peacocks. They lived in Connecticut and had never heard such a sound. They stayed off the deck at night; they left the porch light burning.

Then Jonathan found one dead on the side of the road. At first it looked like someone had tossed a showgirl's costume from a passing car, but he could see the wings when he got up close, the broad breast of iridescent green. Jonathan knew that this was the animal disturbing their evenings. It was too exotic to be otherwise. He wanted one of the tail feathers so that he could show his wife, but he had to step on the bird and pull with both hands in order to get it out.

Back at home, Karen marveled at the giant eyeball at

the end, how it shimmered in the light, how easily it could be damaged. That evening, there was only one peacock calling in the woods, and it seemed to be drifting farther. Jonathan stepped off of the deck and walked down to the edge of the yard. He tried to see it among the trees, but of course there were only shadows getting deeper, the first stars waiting somewhere in the sky. He took a few steps in, then turned to wait for Karen. But she was just settling down, a glass of wine in hand, a breeze from the east rearranging her hair.

A PERFECT ASS

You were staring at my ass, weren't you?

Do you ladies really think I can't see you mentally peeling the jeans away from my bottom, watching in anticipation as I bend down for my briefcase before heading to catch my train? I know what's going on behind your upraised copies of *Marie Claire* and *The Economist*.

It's hard to live with an ass like this, if you want to know the truth. Sure, all I have to do is take off my overcoat and do a little twirl for the hostess, and right away I've got my pick of the tables at any restaurant on a Saturday night. But it's as much a curse as it is a blessing.

Do you think it's easy not knowing if I'm the assistant to the director of purchasing because my boss believes I'm tuned into the fashion world—or because I'm a trophy, a piece of eye candy, something she can take along to meetings to make the other directors drool? Believe me, I know what that sounds like, but come on. If I came to your meeting, it would be like watching a Rolls-Royce pull into your driveway.

When you've got somebody with my caliber of ass working for you, it has ripple effects. People start to wonder, "Why is *he* working for *her?* She must have something going on beneath those panel skirts and culottes. Someone with a great ass like his would never stick with her unless he had to....And why would he have to?" It's a simple equation: The better the ass, the better the fortunes of everyone around it.

As you can imagine, it's a plague of dropped pencils at work. So transparent. I see the women sneaking looks in the lobby mirror as they hold the door for me like we're at a Sadie Hawkins dance. And don't think for a moment I don't know why my mail slot is so close to the floor.

Sometimes I have to travel for work, and I've learned to dread the hotel pools. Even when I don my baggiest trunks, I have to deal with the hush spreading over the lounge chairs as I glide through the cerulean depths like a kingfish. I can understand why. As I hoist myself out onto the lip of the pool in the gathering gold of the afternoon sun, I can feel the wetness defining me like Vermeer's brush.

And when I take the train into work, I can sense the women—and sometimes even the men—jockeying for position as I collect my tablet and my Greek yogurt and my Tupperware of chopped cucumbers. They all want the seat I'm about to vacate, so they can feel the warmth of my derriere rising to embrace them in that cradle of industrial-strength vinyl.

I wear thongs, so you could say I'm my own worst enemy. But who wants to see the outlines of somebody's briefs inside a pair of chinos? For me, at least, it's like putting a shopping mall in Yellowstone or adding a moustache to one of Degas' ballerinas.

But look at those guys over there—folding their pizza so they can fit still more of it into their chomping maws. I can imagine them slathering butter on every millimeter of available bagel. I can imagine them opting for the corner piece of cake and all the frosting that entails. They don't care about the dismal state of their asses, and yet there's a bovine happiness about them. It cannot be denied. From where I stand, quietly doing my clenches, it looks like they have nothing to be happy about. And yet they guffaw and slap their knees, they refuse to napkin up their grease.

It's gotten me to thinking. You hear stories about the rich giving everything away and going to live in the woods. Or beautiful women suddenly deciding to let their hair go gray. Why do they do it, and how do they later meet the world with earnest smiles? The cynic in me wants to say it's because their asses gave out. Or maybe they looked at their parents and saw their future—a calculated surrender.

Or maybe there really is something more to life than money and fashion and callipygian delights.

I've decided to make some changes. So go ahead, ladies. Get a good look at it while you can. In fact, give it a poke with your index finger—like you're late for a party on the 43rd floor. It's pure muscle. I could open champagne with these cheeks.

But starting today, I'm having a donut at every meal. I'm dropping out of my Zumba class. I'm buying a bigger TV. It's a brave new world out there, and I stand upon its precipice, poised to enter the less complicated existence of people with lousy asses.

Don't shake your heads. I know what I hear. How

many times have I left a room and paused upon the threshold as somebody whispered "Unbelievable!" or "Look at that guy—a perfect ass"?

HELEN

Every man in the office wanted to help, but Helen raised a hand to hold us off. She was the best-looking woman on our floor, and all the men—I'm sure of it—had fantasized about cozying up behind her. This was our chance. One of us would get to Heimlich his way into her good graces, to ball his fist and thrust it upward into her diaphragm—quite likely lifting her off the ground, feeling, purely out of circumstance, the cloven jeans against him. There were a dozen of us at the ready, and I remember thinking it implausible that this many people had first-aid training. We jockeyed for position. I tried to make myself wider to retain my place in the tightening knot of men that had surrounded her. Helen's hand came up again, more emphatically this time. "She's still breathing," said one of the secretaries. "Give her some room." Another agreed and cautioned that we might make matters worse. The circle of men loosened—each of us watching the secret muscles of her throat as they tried to end her gurgling. And then she coughed in earnest. The Dorito came back. People clapped. And Helen broke free of our disintegrating ring, hurrying off to compose herself behind the frosted panes of her office—the same panes that kept us from staring at her as we made our trips to the coffee pot. The men went back to their spreadsheets. The ships we had launched lay at the bottom of the harbor, the gulf between us and Helen uncrossable once again.

BAD MANNERS

Carol jumped off this bridge. She held a bag of groceries as she did it. It was foggy, like tonight, and she ended up airborne before she'd gotten over water. That's how I know about the groceries. The morning found her surrounded by broken squash and a box of melted popsicles. The receipt was in her pocket.

It's not a method I recommend. The acceleration must be thrilling, but the sidewalk has its problems. Better to find one of those scenic canyons the base jumpers use or a cliff beside the ocean—someplace that won't need to be pressure-washed. It's inconsiderate of the people who clean up after.

Same thing with Hemingway and Plath—full of despair and, apparently, bad manners.

I doubt Carol bothered calling the 800 number I keep finding on the signs. She was averse to confiding in strangers. She would have felt bad for making the operator think he'd failed her. At least there's that.

The police found Carol's car in the Food Lion parking lot. She must have walked from the cashier to the bridge without dropping off her bag. She was not one to litter so she took it with her over the railing.

Like the rest of them, she didn't think ahead.

The suicides accumulate. They are discovered in garages and underneath bridges and beside their fathers' guns. Somebody always cleans them up. Somebody turns off the car and cracks a window. Somebody tries to keep the children back.

THE PROOFREADER IN HIM
DOESN'T THINK SO

He returns again to the Dalí painting where the insects have only four legs each. He can almost forgive these tiny ants, but even the grasshopper is missing the middle pair. Are four-legged insects the same as melting clocks and burning giraffes? The proofreader in him doesn't think so. He waits for the guard to step away, and then he adds the legs in with a smuggled pen. It is no different than correcting the typos in one of Hemingway's posthumous works, he says to himself. The world can always be more, the pentimento erased. Just yesterday, for example, a storm toppled the trees around his house to tell him the stars still burn.

OUTAGE

They had been quarreling for an hour when they reached a lull, the way a climber reaches a ledge. They sat on the living room couch—the woman staring at the window, the man focused on the carpet—as the radio leaked its message from another room. It was the kind of jazz he didn't understand, the kind of jazz she loved. It was barely there, like the smell of dinner in the house when the dishes are cleared away. The hush had lasted for almost a minute when the power went suddenly out.

Night had fallen hours before, so they found themselves in darkness. They didn't look for a flashlight because each kept thinking the power would come right back, that it was only the wind in the wires. There was no way they could know that a small plane had crashed into a substation and caused a fire, and that it would be many hours, quite possibly days, before their power was restored, before the jazz that had brought them this far could be resumed.

So each continued to sit, the last notes of the horn solo fresh in their minds and fading—one certain of where it would end, the other unsure it had even begun. They refused to look for matches. They left the candles in their drawer. They sat in the center of their pitch-black town and the starlight had its say.

MARINA DAWN

She didn't need to cup her hand around the cigarette. His sails would be useless today, and people would talk if she didn't leave soon. Her feet felt certain as soon as she disembarked.

THE LAST MAN OUT

We worried that they knew, even as they rolled us inside the gates. We imagined the secret order spreading through the streets—to bring torches and straw, to gather up the children so they could watch.

Ajax was the only one who could tell what was going on. He was positioned inside the head, and he peeked through a tiny hole in the horse's left nostril to check on what was happening. Of course, he couldn't risk even a whisper. He had to stay unmoving in the stallion's head, while I sat back in the rear.

A celebration developed. Barrels were produced, the bones of our comrades pulled apart and burned. There was singing and the whores were busy. We heard the children playing about the horse's legs. We heard their glee as they stepped outside the walls for the first time in years.

Helen made a speech. We knew her voice. It filled us with longing and treachery.

Eventually the hairline spaces between the boards filled up with dark. The torches died down. We heard the gates pulled shut with the straining of the yaks, which the boys encouraged by dangling an apple smeared in honey before them.

As we had planned, we waited a whole hour after hearing the last noise. Then we unfolded ourselves from the cramped places our bodies had molded into. The secret door in the belly was pulled back and a rope fell down into dark. One by one the men slid out like spiders. We could see nothing. We followed each other's stink.

I was the last man out. By the time I touched the ground, the guards' drunken throats had been slit and the gates were being drawn. We made a game of going from house to house and killing in quiet the ones who slept. We were searching for Helen, for we would have to take her back—even after she had caused us to murder at close range the families so like our own.

MIDNIGHT

Two of Luke's friends peeked in through a back window. They began clapping. A minute later, Mandy hurried to the car, her shirt buttons misaligned.

LOVE LETTER

Why didn't you keep the flowers? Even if you didn't like them, you could have brought them to the office. That Marjorie always has a sour look on her face. You could have said they were from you. Instead, I had to watch the deliveryman take my bouquet of asters and ox-eye daisies back to his idling van—the tailpipe of which was slowly blackening the snow piled up by your curb.

I might as well tell you I've been watching. I can see you staring at the phone in your bedroom as my voice comes out of it. I want to talk to you, but not like that.

When you get home, you often leave the curtains open, and I content myself with watching your household routines. Later, I see you reach for the venetian blinds. You let them fall with a thump onto the sill, but they're always a little crooked. I can see your pants darting back and forth in that little corner on the lower right side. I like that about you—you don't feel the need to make everything perfect.

Eventually, the living room lights go off. Then the

bedroom's. That's when I feel there's no reason to stay up. Of course, if you went to the bathroom, I'd still be able to see the top of your head as you sat on the toilet, but it's hard to muster that kind of stamina, night after night.

I'm worried about sending this letter. You're liable to say I'm crowding you, that I don't understand boundaries. I've heard that before. But seriously, if you just picked up the phone when I called and asked about my day, you'd see that I'm alright. I just want to hear your voice as I sit here in my underwear thinking of fonder times—back when we were a couple, when we were taking on the world.

I know what you'll say to that—that we were never a couple, that I was just some guy you met in the grocery store, that I read your address off the check you were writing and then rented a room on the other side of the street—all so I could watch you do the dishes and straighten up your knick-knack shelf.

Let's be honest. You're not dating anyone. At least I've never seen a man stay over, and as best as I can tell, you always come home. I suppose you could be having some kind of fling in the afternoons, but that doesn't seem likely. You work and you come home, and your errands consist entirely of banking and groceries and Pilates.

Well, since you're probably wondering now: Yes, that was me who jumped behind the trash can when you went into Fitness World at 7:57 on Tuesday night. I didn't want to spook you. I had noticed you lingering in front of the flower shop, and when I went up to the window, so that I might touch the fog of your breath upon the glass, I saw the vases full of asters and ox-eye daisies.

I'll be watching as you read this. If you want me to call, just come to the window and wave.

HORNETS

While Magda slept, her faucet leaked hornets. One by one they plopped into the dirty basin of her bathroom sink, wet with the water of the secret pipes that came from under the city.

Each hornet flew off into the darkened house, touching down in a box of love letters that sat on the kitchen table. Magda had betrayed each of the letter writers, and she had been up late regretting her decisions. The last of the burgundy sat in her glass like a contact lens of blood.

As the hornets landed, the moisture transferred to the letters on which they stood, forming a tiny stain, which the hornets set about chewing, reconstituting the paper into a serviceable pulp. By morning, they had consumed all of the letters, and the nest hung down, impaled on an arm of the chandelier.

When she woke, Magda heard the low buzzing of the nest, but couldn't imagine what it might be. It sounded vaguely electrical, and as she walked down the hall, a hornet passed her, hugging the ceiling. She saw how its wings pushed the cobwebs around that the maid had failed to remove. She followed it into the kitchen.

The nest became aroused by her presence. The hornets ricocheted off the walls and cabinets. They began landing on Magda's legs and hair. They crawled up her nightgown. From afar, they resembled a terrifying jewelry.

Magda burst out the front door, pulling her nightgown off as she ran. She moved through the yard in a straight line, toward what she did not know, but it seemed foreordained. When she collapsed on the lawn, naked, she was not far from her neighbor who was warming up his car in the November frost.

And then the hornets left her, like berries on a bush overtaken by birds whose hunger was strong and righteous.

THE RECIPE CALLED FOR VINEGAR

In June, as Timothy toured the farm on his first day of work, Mrs. D'Angelo pointed out the black walnuts rising beside the creek. She told him she had the same kind of trees in her yard growing up, and when she was fifteen, she'd collected the nuts all morning and threw them into her father's trout pond, to see if the fish would really die. By dinnertime, the trout were swimming sideways, rolling their bellies into the pastel air. When she returned the next morning with a pool skimmer, Mrs. D'Angelo found the St. Croix rod where her father had dropped it. "That was the first time he used a belt," she said.

The creek divided the D'Angelo's blueberry fields from a horse farm on the other side, and the horses would gather beneath the walnut trees as the wind got hot and the berries fell apart if you kept on picking. Mrs. D'Angelo tasted one from the last bush in the row, and a horse walked down to get a drink.

"Do those horses ever cross?" Timothy asked.

Mrs. D'Angelo didn't answer. She was prone to silences, and often seemed to be concentrating on something far away. She was a good-looking woman though, and Timothy didn't mind walking behind her, waiting for whatever she would tell him next. Her husband, Carmen, was different. He talked steadily about the task at hand, and he had a way of clapping Timothy on the shoulder, at the end of a conversation, that made him think of his own father. Sometimes, Carmen would come over to the blueberry field and tell his wife he needed Timothy, and that would be the end of Timothy's picking.

One day, Carmen and Timothy stood opposite each other with the grape vines in between them. They looked funny like that. They each had the same head of wild black hair. Together they harvested the purple clusters, pulling them off in clumps and dropping them into the large bucket each wore on a sling across his shoulder.

That's when Carmen told Timothy about his testicular cancer. "It was a couple of years ago. They took everything," he said. Timothy imagined the terrible smoothness of Carmen's naked body. "I'd probably blow my brains out if I was your age," he said, passing over a fistful of grapes with too much green.

Carmen kept picking as if he'd just said something about the weather. That was Carmen. He was always direct, but it was harder for Timothy. The whole farm was washed in light that day, and the plowed dirt of the fallow field behind Carmen was starting to get covered by a fine patina of weeds. Timothy wished he had said something back.

If Timothy wasn't helping Carmen, he'd be over by Imogene. She was one of the pickers who spoke English and had worked on the farm for many years. "My dumbass husband had quite a time last night," she said to the air. Timothy looked up and she caught it. "He was driving home from the bar, coming down Route 71. Probably speeding." Imogene sucked on her cigarette then, and squinted one eye as she did it—like she was looking at the world through a gunsight.

"All of a sudden he sees this white swoop shoot down in front of the truck and there's a thud, so he pulls over to see what it was. Stuck in the grill is an owl—a barn owl, white as a bride and bloody." Imogene lifted a branch and peered in to assess the berries. "He figured it was dead, but when he tried to pull it out, the owl went crazy. Tore him up good. That beak is like pliers made of razor blades."

"What happened?" Timothy asked. Imogene looked at him hard and flicked her cigarette still smoking into a blueberry row where some of the Mexicans were picking. "To the owl, I mean."

"He got the jack handle and beat the shit out of it. Then he drove to the hospital to get his stitches." The two of them watched a meadowlark float by on the wind. "That's what he said anyway."

Back at Timothy's mother's house, Timothy and his girlfriend, Evelyn, got high and stuffed themselves on berries. Timothy brought home a pint of them every day and they decided to bake a pie. He was surprised when Imogene's handwritten recipe called for vinegar. He thought it might be a mistake, but when they broke into the finished pie for a taste, Evelyn said, "I *told* you it'd be alright."

Timothy and Evelyn had been dating for a few months. Timothy had fallen hard for her, and when he would leave for the blueberry farm at 5:30 a.m., he would drive by Evelyn's house, even though it wasn't on the way. Her window would be black, and he'd think of her burrowed into the blankets as the cool air tumbled in and the sound of his bad power steering drifted over her. That summer, she worked as an intern in some office park and could afford the extra sleep, but it was still a little dark as Timothy took the long dirt driveway up to the farm. There wasn't any dust in the rearview because of the dew, but when he drove back home at noon, the dust rose up and followed like a tiny storm.

Timothy got out of the car, and as often as not, he'd see a meadowlark standing on a fence post, singing to the blueberries. He figured it must be the same one each morning. Its belly was bright yellow and it had a black collar. He thought it looked fake—like someone had cinched a loop around its neck to keep it on that fence. All the spiderwebs were visible at that hour, strung between the rows and heavy with dew, or forming unlikely tunnels into the grass almost everywhere he looked. It made him worry about what he couldn't see in broad daylight when the dew had burned away.

When July rolled around, Timothy and Carmen were connecting irrigation pipe in anticipation of a dry patch. They were in the field that butted up against Grove Avenue when a pickup truck pulled over to them. It had a piano strapped into the bed. The driver leaned out and asked Carmen if he could point him to Castle Hill Road. Carmen wiped his forehead and explained that the driver needed to get on the other side of town. It was complicated. All the while, Timothy kept dragging the pipe sections into place and snapping them together. When the driver had what he needed, he raised his voice a little so that Timothy could overhear and said, "Tell your son to keep up the good work." As he pulled away, Carmen laughed, "He's the son I'll never have." Timothy laughed too, but he felt bad about it later, as he recounted the story to Evelyn.

One afternoon, Carmen was pushing a wheelbarrow full of horseshit over to a new row of grapes. He looked substantial. The sweat poured out of him like everything was working. His vines had all come from Sicily, from the vineyard where the Rovittello was made that he and Mrs. D'Angelo drank just before kissing for the first time. Carmen told Timothy all about it, but nobody else knew. He wanted to make one barrel of perfect wine. Then he could die. That's what he said.

"We're at the same latitude as where these grapes are grown on the slopes of Mt. Etna," Carmen said. "The sunlight, the angle of the sun, that's the hard part." He flattened a clod of dirt with the heel of his boot. "With the soil, it's just a matter of mixing in enough ash and manure."

Timothy looked a few years into the future, and saw Carmen and Mrs. D'Angelo sitting down to that first good bottle—how she would look across the candlelight and say that it tasted familiar. What a move, he thought. A long-range plan, a guaranteed lay. Then Timothy remembered about Carmen.

Each workday ended with Timothy in the packing shed smoking a cigarette after filling the truck with the day's berries. Carmen took the whole load into town, and Mrs. D'Angelo went up to the house for lunch. Timothy liked to stand there with the smoke curling around his fingers and look out over the fields as if they were his own. The meadowlarks had disappeared by then, probably to the deep shade along the creek.

That's when Timothy saw a man step out of the berries beside the house, and walk in through the back door without knocking or even pausing. At first, he thought he must be using the toilet, but there was a Port-a-Potty out by the barn and everybody knew to pee in the creek.

This happened at least once a week, sometimes more. Then, one day, deep into summer, Timothy was standing beside Imogene when the same man came out of the rows and walked inside the house. He could see her watching, and he asked her who he was. Timothy said it nonchalantly, but Imogene understood.

"That's Mr. Morris," she said. "He owns the farm on the other side of the creek."

"The guy with the horses?" he asked.

Imogene shook a cigarette out of her pack, lighting it as she waited for the next question. When it didn't come, she inhaled and squinted. "Carmen knows all about it. He's a good man," she said.

It was hard for Timothy to look at Carmen after that. He seemed like a fool. Timothy did his best to avoid him and his odd jobs, but he couldn't put his heart into berry picking either. He started filling fewer buckets, and he didn't care if some green berries got mixed in. Mrs. D'Angelo noted everything and lectured him about his lateness.

"The berries wait for no man," she said as she punched the card of a Mexican about Timothy's age, who hustled back into his row. "I need people who can empty this field before the birds do."

Timothy was sure she hadn't fired him because of

Carmen, but part of Timothy wished she would just get it over with. He couldn't stop thinking about the wine of their first kiss—from before they'd had a chance to contemplate mortgages and cancer. Now that Timothy knew about Mr. Morris, the whole thing seemed depressing. The taste of that wine was supposed to say something like harvest—endless and abundant—at least to Timothy. It was meant to recall that happy time when they felt disoriented and didn't know where to look in the world because every part of it seemed beautiful.

It was the way, Timothy thought, that he and Evelyn were feeling—a careless kind of love. They had another year of high school left. They hadn't yet thought about college or careers. Evelyn was on the pill, and Timothy couldn't get over the way she held onto his back as they made love—like she was afraid she'd fly away, like she needed Timothy to anchor her. He saw the years stretch out before him, and tried to imagine a circumstance in which he would encourage her to screw the horse farmer next door.

One day, Timothy found himself alone with Mrs. D'Angelo. She was busy with some oily part that had to be adjusted or replaced. "Someday they'll invent a machine that will pick these berries for me," she said. "Then I won't have to rely on high school kids and immigrants to get the job done right." She said this without heat as she tried to fit one part inside another. It was just a fact.

"You remember that story about the walnuts?" he asked. "The one with your father's pond?"

Mrs. D'Angelo put down the part and began searching the work table for a rag to wipe her hands.

"Why did you do it? Why did you want to kill your

father's fish?" The question surprised them both. It had the quality of a doorbell being rung in a house where there was no doorbell.

"I was angry," she said. "He told me I couldn't go to the dance with a boy I liked—because he was older, because he rode a motorcycle." She gazed up at the slats of light coming through the barn ceiling as she said this.

"It was a stupid thing to do," she said. "My father loved that little pond. He'd go out there and cast a bit after dinner when he was in a mood, and when he came back in, he'd always sound better."

"What happened after?" Timothy asked.

"Oh, I went to the dance with the boy anyway. It wasn't hard for me to fool my old father," she said.

Timothy was silent. He looked at the parts spread out on the table in front of Mrs. D'Angelo and couldn't figure out what kind of machine it was.

"Just you wait," she said. "Someday you'll meet a girl and you'll be surprised how dumb you can be." Then she went back to fussing with the disassembled machine.

By August, Timothy was up in the packing shed with a letter for Mrs. D'Angelo. He'd been carrying it all week in his shirt pocket, and he was starting to think he'd have to retype it, out of respect for Carmen. Timothy had just put the last of the crates into the truck bed, and he slapped the side to let Carmen know the job was done. Carmen pulled out and Timothy saw his nod in the rearview.

Timothy lit a cigarette and thought about how farm life wasn't for him after all. For one thing, the day ended too early. When Timothy got home at one o'clock, Evelyn was still at the office, and he'd putter and doze, unable to concentrate. He had started watching soap operas to fill the time. Then, when he finally saw Evelyn, she was full of stories from the office—the gossip that Lori, another intern, brought to her each morning like a pastry, the funny thing that Doug, her boss, had said to her as they chatted over lunch.

"This place is just full of shit," he said aloud, and flicked his cigarette out on the crushed stone that covered the ground around the shed. He thought about how the stone used to be a mountainside, how people had invented machines that could turn it into driveways all over Arkansas.

"Ain't it though," said Imogene.

Timothy jumped. He hadn't known she was sitting behind him among the empty packing crates. She squinted and laughed, and he turned back around more quickly than he wanted to.

Carmen's truck was getting smaller as he passed the grapes he was turning into wine, the dust following as he headed into town. He was almost invisible from where Timothy stood, and then he saw Mrs. D'Angelo climbing the steps of her porch. He stayed there for a moment, listening for meadowlarks but hearing only wind as it crawled along the creek—beside a field still pushing out berries, among the walnuts full of poison.

THE PACKING UP

We never heard a sound coming from our neighbors, who were separated from us by thick walls of forsythia. Still, whenever we made love, Denise insisted on closing the windows. She would even lock the bedroom door, though we had no children, not even a cat that could nose its way inside. Later, when we had stopped making love altogether, the house held our silence like a broken bell. Anyone listening as they let their dog pee against our mailbox would be unable to guess whether ours was a house of passion or devastation. Even the packing up was quiet.

SOMEBODY WHO KNOWS SOMEBODY

I spot George at the airport bar in Chicago, waiting for his potato skins to arrive. Our planes on the way to Connecticut have been grounded and the place is packed. Bad weather has brought us together.

At first I don't believe the story but George insists. Joanne is his sister after all, and why would he lie? Several times a day, he says, Joanne slips off into the back bedroom to use a breast pump. She unbuttons her shirt and unsnaps her bra and sits on a little black stool. Over each breast she places the plastic shields that look like translucent trumpet bells. Then she switches the pump on with her big toe. For some reason, George tells me the nail is yellow.

The soft whirring of the machine is pleasant enough for Joanne, but after a couple of minutes her nipples begin to ache. Over and over, she sees them pulled and let go by the suction of the machine. There is no milk yet. Joanne has never even been pregnant. Sometimes she cries because, after her fifteen-minute session, she will remove the shields and see that her nipples are cracked and bleeding.

As she's pumping, Joanne stares at a photograph of a newborn baby swaddled in the hospital blanket all babies seem to enter the world in—a kind of uniform, fitting as snugly as darkness inside of an unused room. The baby belongs to a woman named Melissa. Melissa will be dead soon—a couple of weeks at most. That's what the doctors say. That's why Joanne is getting the baby.

Everyone says Joanne is crazy. They say this behind her back, of course, but she can tell. An unmarried 44-year-old woman who has never had kids telling her co-workers that she'll have a new baby in two weeks, and that she intends to breastfeed, doesn't sound level-headed. Especially because it will be the baby of a dead stranger.

Joanne doesn't care. She goes into the back bedroom. She uses the lactation room at work. She takes vitamins and supplements and stares at the baby's picture taped to the breast pump motor. The baby's name is Alex, for the man who left Melissa when he found out how sick she was. That's the kind of sob story this is. Melissa has entered the hospice. She is in a coma that, stubbornly, will not progress, and she has named her baby after a douchebag.

As George and I talk over our beers, he tells me that, at this moment, his mother is driving north from South Carolina with Alex in a car seat, crying. She is bringing back the baby for Joanne because Joanne can't afford to take off from work. The money is just too tight, now that she's been buying the baby stuff, now that she has paid off the sister of Melissa—a woman named Grace. Melissa had wanted Grace to take over, but Grace is full of bad habits. She knows she can't care for the baby, and the adoption was arranged by church members who found a common, tenuous tie between Melissa and Joanne. Before she slipped into the coma, Melissa had two dying wishes. The first was that George's mother take Alex back to Connecticut right now. They had already filled out the paperwork, and Melissa worried that Grace would have second thoughts, that Alex might end up in the care of strangers. The second wish was that her baby not fly in an airplane.

"George," I say. "Isn't she scared to take this on by herself, at her age?" I finish my beer and raise my fingers so the barkeep will bring us more, even though George tries to say he's good.

"The situation is not optimal," he says. That's George. He's an engineer, and he sees everything in terms of the likelihood of failure, the chances of continuing from the present point in time.

"It's funny," he says. "A comatose woman in South Carolina knows somebody who knows somebody, who knows a childless woman in Connecticut desperate to adopt." He goes to sip his beer but puts it back down, looking at me in the mirror behind the bar. "It's right on the border of not even being a connection."

I'm not sure what to say to that, but I clink my bottle into both of his because if nothing else is clear, at least George is an uncle now.

George's food arrives, and we make some room in front of us on the bar. But the potato skins, it turns out, aren't any good. They must have been forgotten and allowed to cool for too long in the busy kitchen.

Then George tells me how Joanne both fears and longs for the milk to come in. She longs for it for the obvious reasons, but also because she believes the earth will spin differently, more meaningfully after it happens. She fears it because the timeline her lactation consultant gave her is the same one Melissa's doctor gave to her. Ten days. 14 at the most.

Joanne stares into the light-intolerant eyes of Alex. She clicks off the breast pump with her yellow toe and checks for milk. She feels the earth flattening out toward the horizon—like Columbus had never set sail, like he'd never even seen a fucking boat. It was a world in which Alex would make his way to her with ease.

And so he was—at 65 miles per hour, with regular stops for diaper changes and formula. Everyone is hoping Alex will miss the storm that has grounded his uncle. Everyone is hoping, despite the odds, that his new mother, who waits with bleeding breasts, will make things right in his corner of the pan-flat world.

ACKNOWLEDGEMENTS

The Light Made Everything Harder to See—*New World Writing*

The Cellist—*Short, Fast, and Deadly*

Bovine and Defenseless—*Razor Literary Magazine*

This Woman Was a Leopard—*Necessary Fiction*

For Official Use Only—*Per Contra*

Ship Inside a Bottle—*The Metaworker*

The Blue Piano—*Juked*

Six Fingers—*Milk Candy Review*

That Cupola Lying on Its Side and Covered in Vines—*New Flash Fiction Review*

Neighbors—*Gravel*

It Would Never Be This Clean Again—*Toasted Cheese*

The First Signs—*Postcard Shorts*

What Have You Done?—*Word Riot*

Flowers—*No Extra Words*

A Brief History of My Relationship With Mercury—*Ink & Coda*

His Glasses—*Blink-Ink*

Medusa—*NANO Fiction*

Romance—*Belle Ombre*

Register 8—*Brilliant Flash Fiction*

My Three-Way—*Microfiction Monday Magazine*

Romulus—*The Metaworker*

Inheritance—*Bending Genres*

Then I Felt the Floor Beneath Me—*Literary Orphans*

An Inability to Focus—*Cease, Cows*

Souderville—*Evening Street Review*

Rhododendron—*The Emerson Review*

Mary and Bernard: A Cautionary Tale—*GNU Journal*
Fling—*Two Sentence Stories*
Colonel Sanders in Extremis—*Cheat River Review*
Because He Had Been Crying—*Cincinnati Review*
The One I Ran Down on Sugar Street—*Cog*
Peacocks—*Paragraphiti*
A Perfect Ass—*Scintilla*
Helen—*Funny in Five Hundred*
Bad Manners—*Juked*
The Proofreader in Him Doesn't Think So—*Okay Donkey*
Outage—*Sequestrum*
Marina Dawn—*Nailpolish Stories*
The Last Man Out—*Juked*
Midnight—*Nailpolish Stories*
Love Letter—*Route 7*
Hornets—*Flash Fiction Magazine*
The Recipe Called for Vinegar—*Better Than Starbucks*
The Packing Up—*The Drabble, Nanoism*
Somebody Who Knows Somebody—*Fiction Southeast*

--

"Medusa" won the 2016 NANO Fiction Prize.
"The Blue Piano" was longlisted for the Wigleaf 50.

ABOUT THE AUTHOR

Charles Rafferty's most recent collection of poems is *The Smoke of Horses* (BOA Editions, 2017). His poems have appeared in *The New Yorker, Gettysburg Review,* and *Ploughshares.* His stories have appeared in *The Southern Review, Juked,* and *New World Writing.* His story collection is *Saturday Night at Magellan's* (Fomite Press, 2013). Currently, he co-directs the MFA program at Albertus Magnus College and teaches at the Westport Writers' Workshop.